TEENAGE MUTANT NINJA TURTLES

TURTLE TALES

An Insider's Guide by Leonardo™
with Jim Thomas
illustrated by Chris George and Mike Giles

Simon Spotlight
New York   London   Toronto   Sydney

Based on the TV series *Teenage Mutant Ninja Turtles*™ as seen on 4KidsTV™

SIMON SPOTLIGHT

An imprint of Simon & Schuster Children's Publishing Division

1230 Avenue of the Americas, New York, New York 10020

Manufactured in the United States of America

First Edition

2 4 6 8 10 9 7 5 3 1

ISBN-13: 978-1-4169-4885-8

ISBN-10: 1-4169-4885-6

Originally published in 2004 as *Turtle Power!: A Scrapbook by Leonardo*™

In the Beginning . . .

Hello! I'm Leonardo, one of the Teenage Mutant Ninja Turtles. And this is my insider's guide to our world.

Let me start at the beginning of our story. Master Splinter found my three brothers and me in the sewer.

We were just regular garden-variety baby turtles back then, walking on four legs and everything. But we were covered in this strange, glowing green ooze. And lying next to us was a broken canister marked with the letters *TCRI*. We still don't know what that means or where the canister came from.

Master Splinter, who was then also an ordinary rat, took us home with him. But that green ooze must have really been something because the next day we all started to change—to mutate!

As the years passed, we all grew much larger than we should have. Eventually we started talking and walking upright—things I understand normal rats and turtles don't do.

Master Splinter named us from a book on Renaissance art: my brothers are Michelangelo, Donatello, and Raphael. Master Splinter also began to teach us the art of ninjitsu, which he learned from his master, Yoshi.

For the last fifteen years we lived happily in our home in the New York City sewers until Mouser robots destroyed it. We've only just found a new place to hang our shells, and it's totally cool!

Home, Sweet, Home . . .

Donatello

Um . . . hi. Donatello here. Leo asked me to write about our new lair.

The first thing I want to say is that it's a complete and utter mystery as to who built it. The walls look like they've been cut from solid rock! And the doors are the weirdest shape. Not to mention the strange glowing crystals we've found all over the place, and the hidden elevator that leads up to the surface.

But none of that changes the fact that the place is totally rockin'.

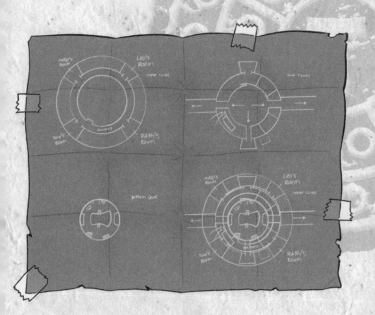

The main chamber is so big we've split it up into different sections. We've got a gym for sparring and working out and a dining room for eating. I even have my own workshop! I'm also building us a monitor wall with lots of TVs wired together and stacked on top of each other.

Everyone gets his own room. Master Splinter's is the largest. It's totally Zen with candles, a paper screen, a meditation mat, and a rock garden.

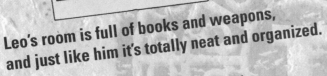

Leo's room is full of books and weapons, and just like him it's totally neat and organized.

Mikey's room is a mess. Comics, cards, DVDs, books, and video games are all over the place.

My room is just as messy, but instead of comics and video games, I have circuit boards and half-finished inventions lying around.

Raph doesn't spend much time in his room, so it's pretty empty. It's the closest to the exit; he often sneaks out to explore aboveground.

There are two access tunnels off the main chamber. One leads to the subway. The other leads to the sewers and the Sewer Slider. Hey, I might as well talk about our kickin' vehicles!

The Battle Wagon

My personal fave. Before I got my hands on it, it was just an armored car. Now it's got:

- a sliding door in the floor
- a roof hatch
- a high-torque winch
- a telescoping satellite dish
- turbo-boosters
- an onboard computer and communications station
- a launch bay for the Shell Cycle
- a kickin' stereo system!

The Shell Cycle

- Put together from the parts of different motorcycles, it's a one-of-a-kind! We keep the Shell Cycle and the Battle Wagon in an abandoned warehouse at the top of the secret elevator.

The Sewer Slider

- Great for getting around in the sewers
- It has a pilot area up front and a cargo area in the rear. Riding on this shock-mounted beauty is like riding an underground roller coaster!

Hey, Michelangelo here. It's about time I got my hands on Leo's little book. Speaking of Leo, how 'bout some interview action with the book's owner?

A-hem! Mr. Leonardo! We just need a moment of your time. Your fans want to know all about you! So would you say you're the unofficial leader of the Brothers Green?

 Leo: Uh, I guess so. But that's only because I'm the best at battle strategy. I keep my head in a fight and make good decisions. Plus I'm always thinking of what's best for the group. I know that when we work together as a team, we're unbeatable!

 Mike: And no one's more serious about training than you are, Brother. For the record here's a page from your training log. Speaking of the Master, do you think he likes you best?

 Leo: Master Splinter loves each of us equally for who we are. But the sensei and I do share an appreciation for the spiritual side of the martial arts.

 Mike: Okay, last question. Your weapons. You're an awesome swords-turtle with your twin katana blades. . . .

 Leo: Yeah, I do love those swords. Master Splinter says that he chose those as my weapons because of my sharp mind and steely resolve.

 Mike: And there you have it! Our fearless leader Leonardo in a nut—I mean, turtle!—shell.

Leo's Training Log

6:00 a.m.	Go for a run through the sewer
7:00 a.m.	Meditation
8:00 a.m.	Breakfast
9:00 a.m.	Workout: calisthenics, weight training, forms practice, lecture and instruction from Master Splinter
1:00 p.m.	Lunch, reading, research, meditation
2:00 p.m.	Workout: weapons practice, sparring
6:00 p.m.	Dinner, consultation with Master Splinter
7:00 p.m.	Workout and cooldown
11:00 p.m.	Meditation
12 midnight	Lights out!

Leo: Okay, Mikey, now it's your turn.

Mike: Hey, that's all right with me. You know how I love the spotlight!

Leo: So, Mike, of the four of us you're probably the most creative. You like to draw, you sketch your own comics, you taught yourself to play guitar, and you like to listen to music. How do you find the time and energy to train?

Mike: I don't! No, that's not true. I love jumping around and flexing my muscles as much as the next Turtle. Well, maybe not as much as you and Raphael . . .

Leo: But for someone who doesn't train as hard, you can definitely hold your own. What about all those practical jokes? Hiding Master Splinter's staff? Gluing my katanas into their sheaths? Using Raphael's sais as toothpicks?

Mike: Yeah, I really caught it for that last one, didn't I? I thought Raph was never going to talk to me again! What can I say? A Turtle's gotta have a little fun, doesn't he?

Leo: Yeah, but wouldn't you say that your imagination has sometimes gotten you into trouble?

Mike: Well, I do have my nunchakus. They're just as flashy as I am, not to mention that they deliver one shell of a clobbering! And I know I can always count on you guys to help me out!

Donatello

Master Splinter

Leonardo

Raphael

Donatello

 Leo: And now, an interview with the brains of the bunch, Donatello! Hey, Donny, ever since we were little you've been taking things apart and putting them back together again, right?

 Don: Yeah. I guess I've always loved to tinker with gadgets.

 Leo: Lucky for us because you've invented some of our most helpful tools. Not just our vehicles, but ultracool gadgets like the Shell Cell and the Turtle-Vision Goggles. What are you working on right now?

 Don: I'm experimenting with something I'm calling a GliderPak. It looks just like a normal, everyday backpack until—*WHAM!*—out pops a hang glider. Perfect for aerial recon.

 Leo: Not to mention catching a game at Yankee stadium, right?

 Don: I prefer Shea myself.

 Leo: Hey, to each his own. What about your weapon, Donny?

 Don: Ah, the bo staff. Simple but dangerous. Master Splinter chose it for me because I'm long on inspiration and stout of heart.

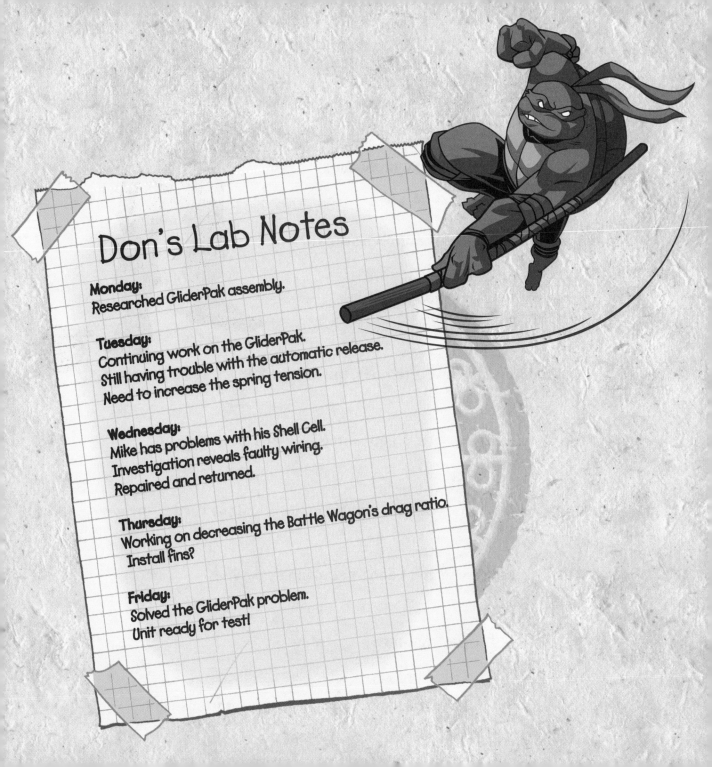

Don's Lab Notes

Monday:
Researched GliderPak assembly.

Tuesday:
Continuing work on the GliderPak.
Still having trouble with the automatic release.
Need to increase the spring tension.

Wednesday:
Mike has problems with his Shell Cell.
Investigation reveals faulty wiring.
Repaired and returned.

Thursday:
Working on decreasing the Battle Wagon's drag ratio.
Install fins?

Friday:
Solved the GliderPak problem.
Unit ready for test!

Raphael

Leo: Last but not least, my hotheaded brother, Raphael.

Raph: Hey! Who you callin' a hothead?

Leo: Are you saying you don't have a temper problem?

Raph: I certainly have a temper, but I don't know if it's a *problem*.

Leo: It's a problem when it gets in the way of your following orders.

Raph: *Your* orders, you mean. Who made you boss Turtle, anyway?

Leo: Okay, okay, you and I don't get along sometimes.

Raph: That's putting it mildly.

Leo: But I got to hand it to you, Raphy. You're a ferocious fighter.

Raph: Yeah, nothing I like better than ten against one. Anything less is too easy!

Leo: That's why Mikey calls you "secret weapon." Hey, how about your twin sais?

Raph: I love 'em. More than a match for your twin katanas.

Leo: If you'll contribute a page of your diary to my scrapbook, I'll meet you in the gym in an hour and we'll see.

Raph: You're on!

Dear Diary,

Another sweltering day in the gym. I kicked some serious shell and was feeling great until Master Splinter took me aside.

I had to spend the next hour in meditation. That was the longest hour of my life! I thought it was never going to end. When it finally did I headed to the surface. I had to get some air. Sometimes I don't know what to do with myself. I guess I'm lucky to have brothers who stand by me even though they drive me crazy sometimes. But where would I be without them?

Master Splinter's Sayings

"Good and evil are choices.
Choose wisely."

"Never sacrifice honor for victory."

"You must see both sides to
understand the whole."

"Practice your moves very
slowly—to execute
them with great speed."

 Leo: Master Splinter is everything to us—our sensei and our father both. After rescuing us he raised us as his own. Master, where did you learn the secrets of ninjitsu?

 Splinter: I learned what I know by watching my owner, a man named Hamoto Yoshi. He was a great master of ninjitsu.

 Leo: What happened to him, Master?

 Splinter: He was murdered by our enemy, Shredder, and his henchman, Hun. Hun is the leader of the Foot and perhaps the worst criminal the world has ever seen. We must ever be wary of him.

April O'Neil and Casey Jones

April and Casey are our two allies from the human world.
They're both part of our family now. Here they are, in their own words:

April: Hey, Casey. You're a vigilante, right? You take justice into your own hands. And in most cases what's in your hands is a baseball bat.

Casey: Goon-gala! That's right, April. Though I do carry a bag with other weapons.

April: Yeah, and you also like to wear a hockey mask. What's with the goofy mask?

Casey: My hockey mask strikes fear into the hearts of the bad guys! Plus it keeps my true identity a secret.

April: Uh-huh. And how about that temper problem of yours?

Casey: It's only a problem for the bad guys. But enough about me. What about you? You're like a big sister to the Turtles.

April: I do what I can. It's not like they can get out and mingle with the rest of the human race. I figure it's up to me to bring them information and supplies, not to mention introducing them to things like Indian food!

Casey: And in return they teach you about the martial arts.

April: That's right.

Casey: You're also smart and have a background in science. No wonder Donatello likes you so much!

April: Don and I speak the same language, no doubt about that.

Casey: Just like me and Raphael.

April: Yep, you both scare me.

Mikey's Comics!!!

Hey, it's me, Mike. I snagged Leo's scrapbook and stuck in these comics. It wouldn't be complete without 'em! Enjoy.

Mikey vs. the Ultimate Ninja!

Written, Penciled, Inked, Colored, and Lettered by Michelangelo

"Show me the one I seek . . . for his end is soon at hand!"

"Young warrior . . . the one called Michelangelo. I have come to this dimension to challenge you to a duel!"

"You picked the wrong guy to challenge, buddy!"

"You lose."   "I . . . I surrender."   "It's so *easy* being green!"

Mikey Hunts the Werewolf!

"AWOOOOOOO!"   "Help!"   "April!"
"Watch out, Mikey! It's a trap!"

"GrrrrOOOOOWWWWLL!"   "Hello, Turtle-man. You think you're going to hurt me with those toothpicks?"
"Hey, dog breath! Why don't you come over here and find out?"

"AIYEEE!"   BAP!   "Help, Mikey!"

"Try this!"   "ARRROOOOOOO!!!"   "My hero!"

We've Met All Kinds . . .

Hey, it's Donny. Here are some of the villains we've met on our adventures. Watch out for 'em!

Shredder

To most of the world Oroku Saki is a wealthy, cultured, and respected Japanese nobleman. But to us he is one of the most powerful criminals— Shredder! A ninjitsu master, Shredder commands a vast criminal organization known as the Foot and wears a suit of multibladed battle armor, which he uses to "shred" his enemies. Master Splinter knows that Shredder is obsessed with finding something— something of great importance to him. But exactly what and why are still a mystery.

Hun

A massive mountain of solid muscle, Hun is Shredder's most trusted henchman. Feared by the Foot, Hun is a deadly combination of physical strength and martial skill. Hun was with Shredder when he murdered Splinter's master. Defending his master, Splinter sprang from his cage and savagely clawed Hun's face. Hun bears the scars to this day.

The Foot

The Foot is a criminal organization whose footprint is rapidly spreading across the world. Their history, traditions, and practices can be traced back to the ancient and mysterious ways of the ninja.
The organization includes:

- **The Ninja Division**—foot soldiers

- **The Tech Division**—developers of new weapons like the FootMechas and the NinjaBorgs

- **The Genetics Division**—bioengineers who create creatures like the SuperSamurai and the SuperSumo

- **The Mystic Division**—investigators of ancient legends, who search for magical and supernatural power

- **The Elite Guard**—Shredder's personal attack force. They are the most dangerous ninjas in the Foot.

Breaking News!

I can't believe it! We've just discovered the truth behind the green ooze that mutated us all those years ago.

We were up on the rooftops when Donny spotted a truck that said "Techno Cosmic Research Institute" on the side. Don wrote out the first letter of each word in the company's name in the dirt—*TCRI*. These were the letters from the canister of green ooze, the ooze that changed us and Master Splinter!

We followed the truck to a building uptown. It's there that we learned answers to questions we hadn't even asked!

Apparently more than a thousand years ago a spaceship crash-landed in Japan. Aboard was a crew of slimy, gumdrop-shaped aliens called the Utrom. These particular Utrom were peacekeepers and had just arrested one of their own . . . a terrible criminal.

Earth at that time didn't have the technology for the peacekeeping Utrom to repair their ship. But they were a very long-lived race. They resolved to wait.

In the meantime they built exoskeletons for themselves that looked like human bodies, so they could blend in. And they formed an alliance with a group of human ninjas, who pledged to protect the Utrom. These protectors were called the Guardians.

The Utrom criminal had escaped after the crash. He knew that if the other Utrom could get home, they would send a force back to recapture him. To prevent that, he had to destroy them. He stole one of their exoskeletons and recruited a band of criminals. These he called the Foot. And as he added armor and blades to his exoskeleton, his army and his enemies began to speak of him fearfully as . . . Shredder!

That's right. Shredder is really a slimy, gumdrop-shaped alien! And there's more. Splinter's owner and master, Hamoto Yoshi, was one of the Utrom's Guardians! The night Shredder killed him, he was trying to get Yoshi to reveal the secret whereabouts of the Utrom. You see, Shredder knows it won't be long before the peacekeeping Utrom manage to adapt the technology they'll need to escape from Earth. He's desperate to find and destroy them before they can!

Parting Thoughts

Master Splinter, my brothers, and I finally know who we are and where we come from. Now it's up to us to make sure the Shredder is defeated once and for all, and our friends, the Utrom, get home. We definitely have our work cut out for us! I can't wait to fill another book with our new adventures!